Q & RAY

CASE #2
METEORITE OR METEOR-WRONG?

TRISHA SPEED SHASKAN

ILLUSTRATED BY STEPHEN SHASKAN

Graphic Universe™ • Minneapolis

Special thanks to Dr. Randy Korotev —TSS and SS

For my nephews Jude and Desmond, the brightest stars, for continually inspiring me. I love you so! —TSS

To Almeida Williams —SS

Graphic Universe™
A division of Lerner Publishing Group, Inc.
241 First Avenue North
Minneapolis, MN 55401 USA

For reading levels and more information, look up this title at www.lernerbooks.com.

Main body text set in CCDaveGibbonsLower 11.5/13.25.
Typeface provided by ComicCraft.

Library of Congress Cataloging-in-Publication Data

Names: Shaskan, Trisha Speed, 1973– author. | Shaskan, Stephen, illustrator.
Title: Meteorite or meteor-wrong! / written by Trisha Speed Shaskan ; illustrated by Stephen Shaskan.
Description: Minneapolis : Graphic Universe, [2018] | Series: Q & Ray ; case #2 | Summary: "Quillan Hedgeson, a hedgehog, and Raymond Ratzberg, a rat, are students (and crime solvers) at Elm Tree Elementary school. When a famous local meteorite goes missing, Q and Ray set out to solve the case, using their wits and a series of disguises" –Provided by publisher. | Includes bibliographical references. | Description based on print version record and CIP data provided by publisher; resource not viewed.
Identifiers: LCCN 2016037376 (print) | LCCN 2017016808 (ebook) | ISBN 9781512451221 (eb pdf) | ISBN 9781512411485 (lb : alk. paper)
Subjects: LCSH: Graphic novels. | CYAC: Graphic novels. | Mystery and detective stories. | Meteorites–Fiction. | Science museums–Fiction. | School field trips–Fiction. | Hedgehogs–Fiction. | Rats–Fiction.
Classification: LCC PZ7.7.S455 (ebook) | LCC PZ7.7.S455 Met 2018 (print) | DDC 741.5/973–dc23

LC record available at https://lccn.loc.gov/2016037376

Manufactured in the United States of America
1-39654-21286-8/2/2017

WHO'S WHO

Quillan Hedgeson
aka: Q

Ray Ratzberg

Mr. Shrew
Media Specialist

Ms. Boar
Classroom Teacher

Principal Badger

Frank Ferret

Ms. Mole

Officer Rocco

CHAPTER ONE
Meteorites Are Mysteries!

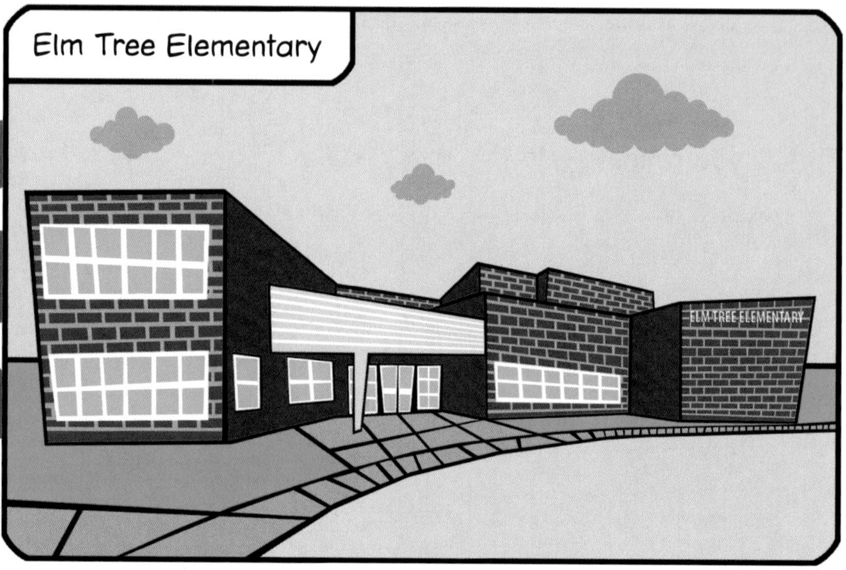
Elm Tree Elementary
ELM TREE ELEMENTARY

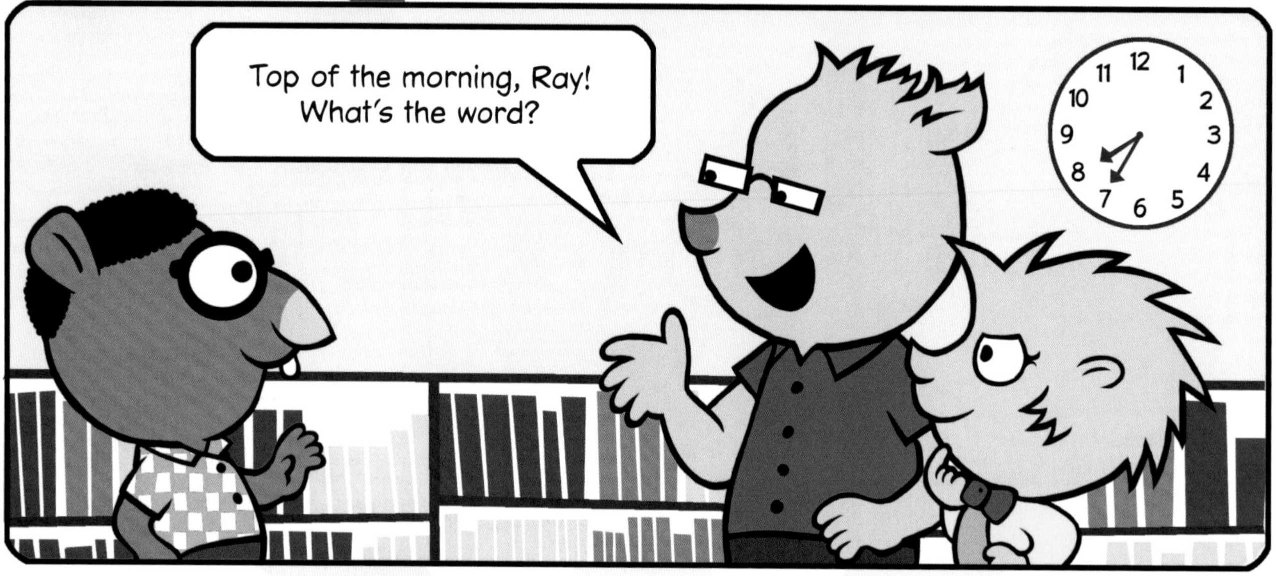
Top of the morning, Ray! What's the word?

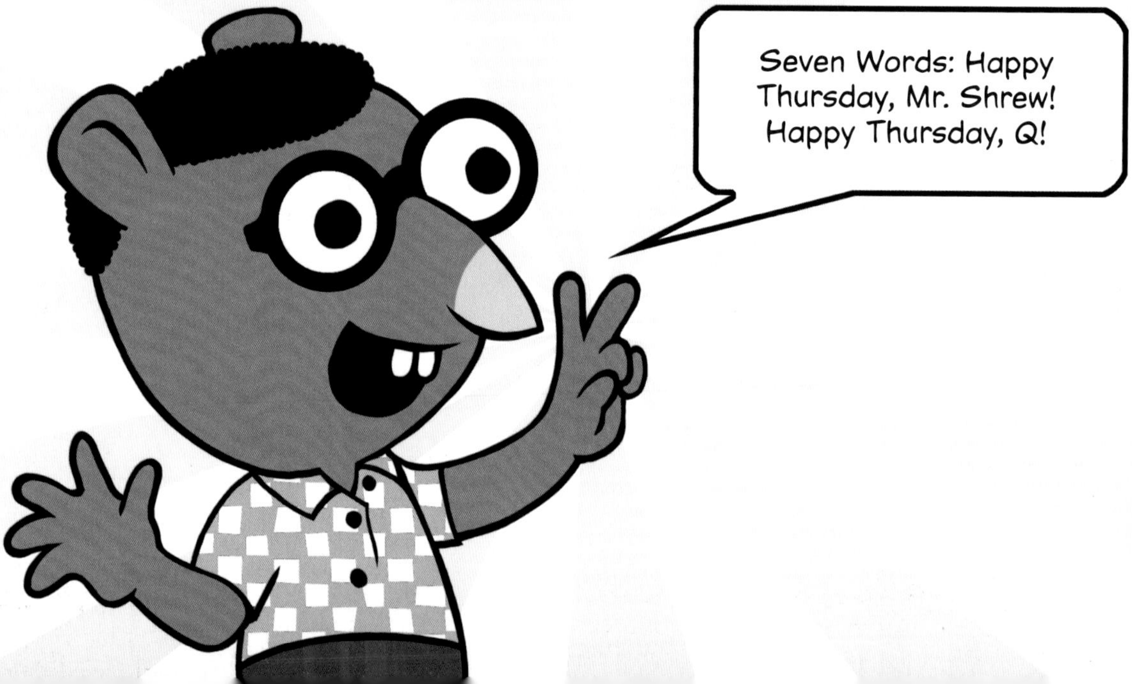
Seven Words: Happy Thursday, Mr. Shrew! Happy Thursday, Q!

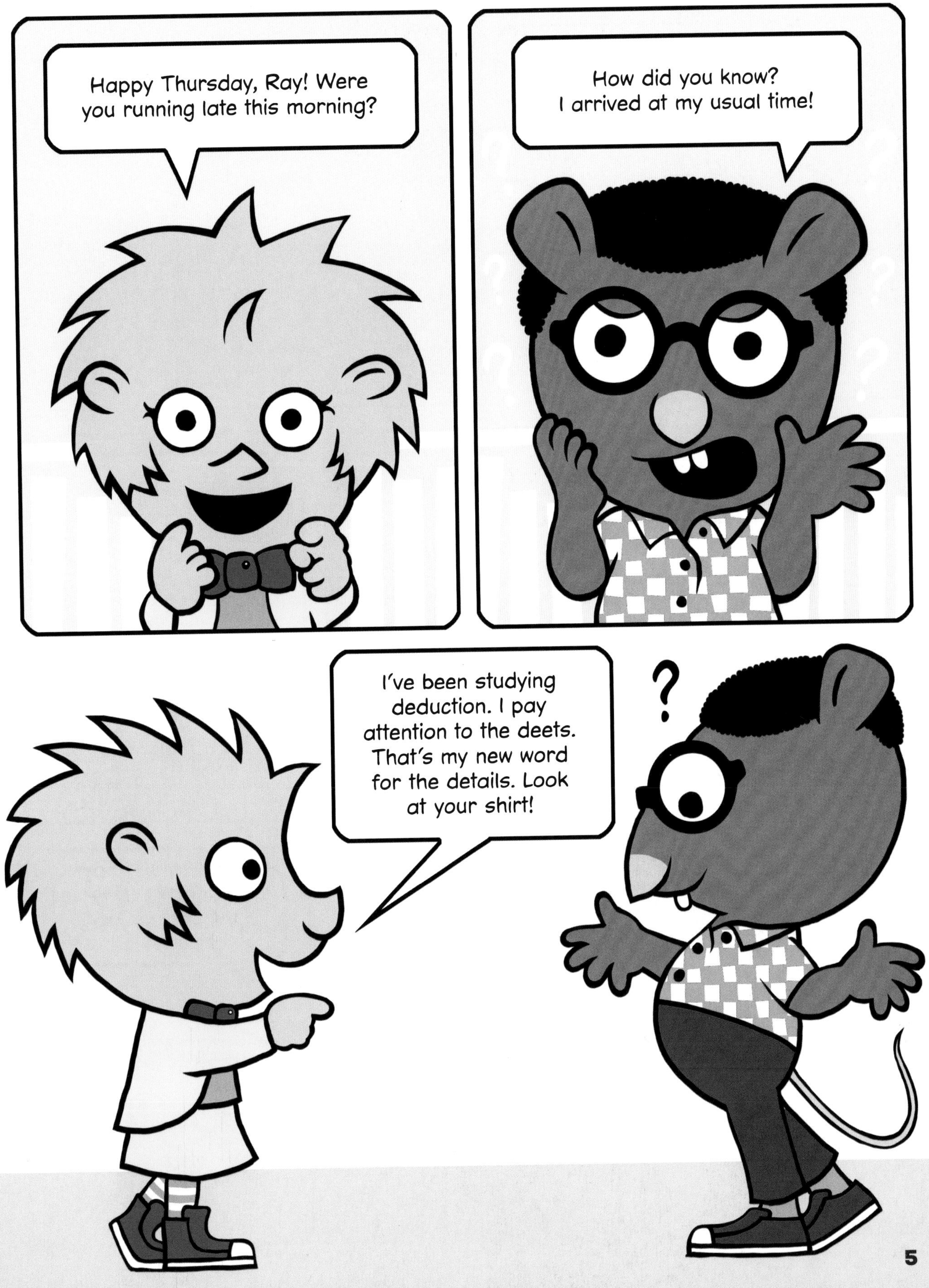
Happy Thursday, Ray! Were you running late this morning?
How did you know? I arrived at my usual time!
I've been studying deduction. I pay attention to the deets. That's my new word for the details. Look at your shirt!
?

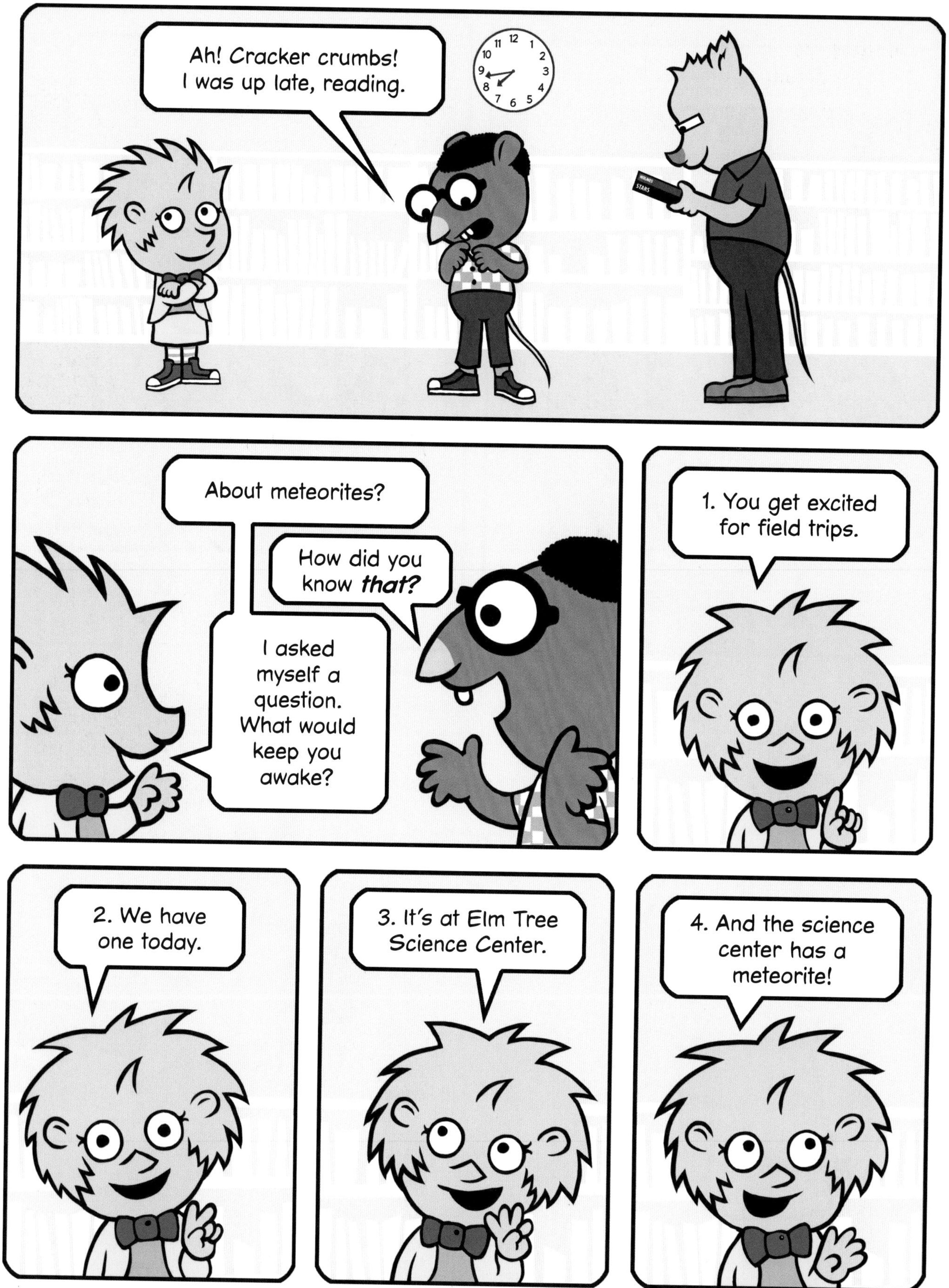
Ah! Cracker crumbs!
I was up late, reading.
About meteorites?
How did you know *that?*
I asked myself a question. What would keep you awake?
1. You get excited for field trips.
2. We have one today.
3. It's at Elm Tree Science Center.
4. And the science center has a meteorite!

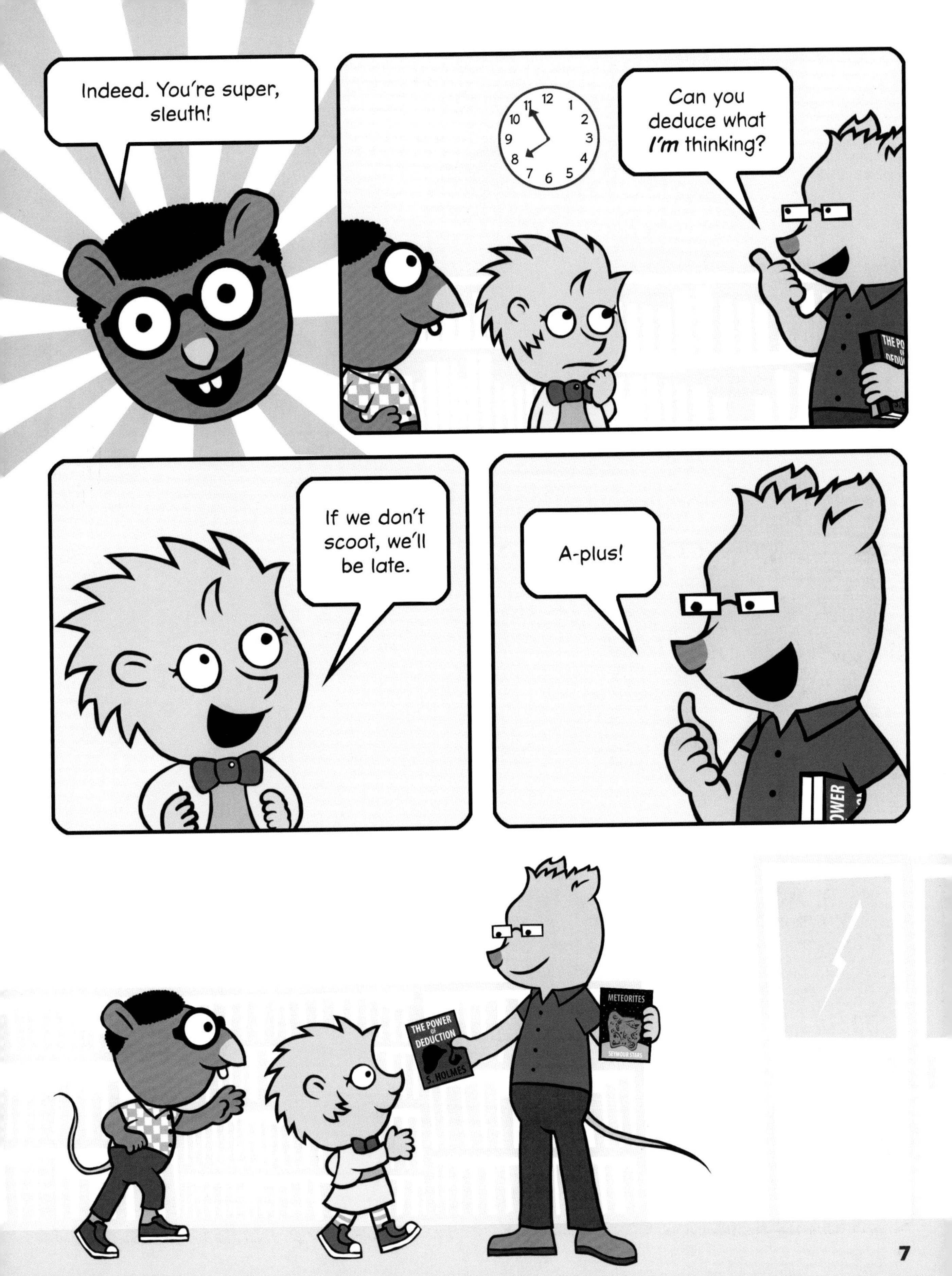

Indeed. You're super, sleuth!
Can you deduce what *I'm* thinking?
THE POWER OF DEDUCTION
If we don't scoot, we'll be late.
A-plus!
POWER
THE POWER OF DEDUCTION
S. HOLMES
METEORITES
SEYMOUR STARS

CHAPTER TWO
Meet Frank Ferret

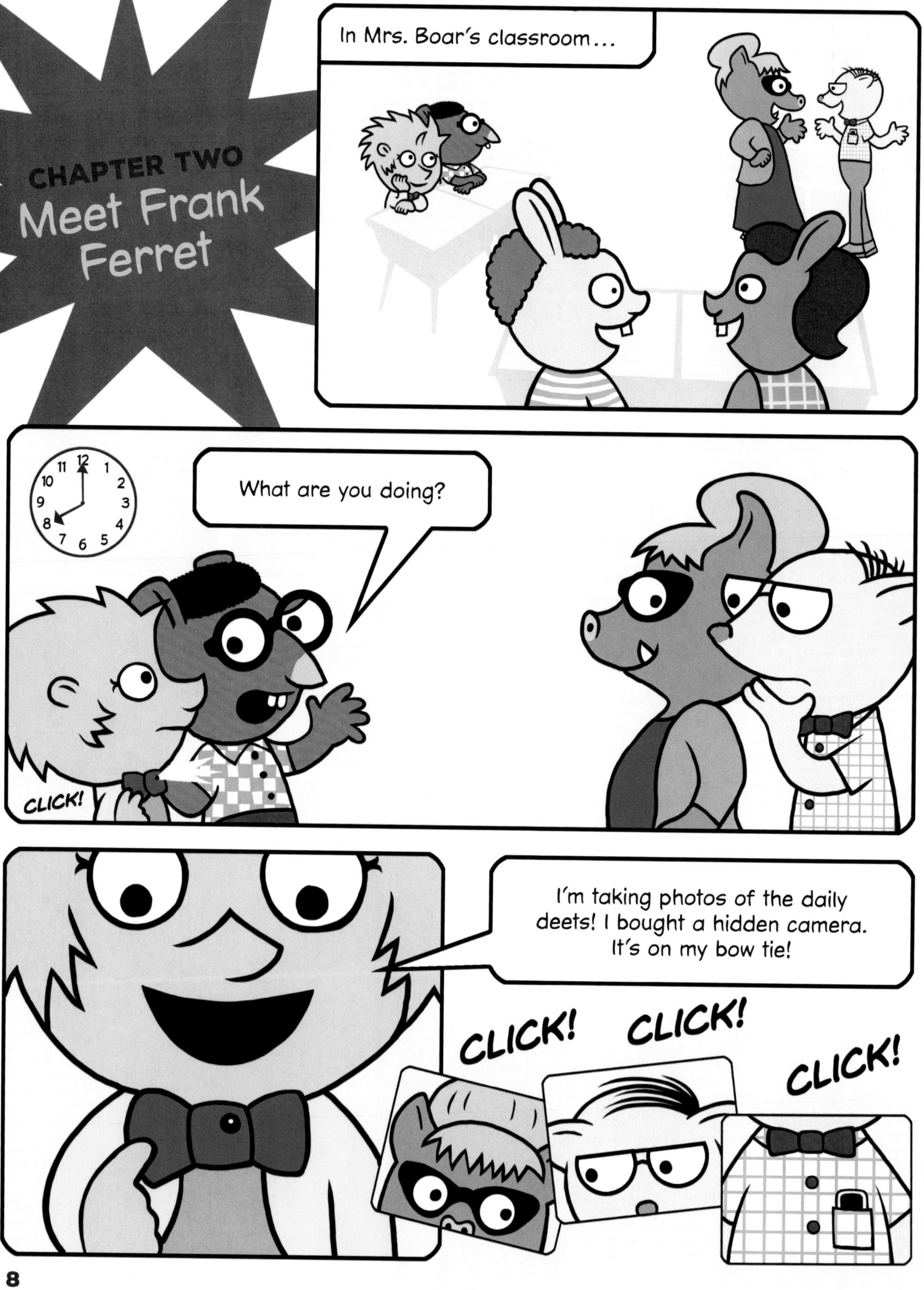

In Mrs. Boar's classroom...
What are you doing?
CLICK!
I'm taking photos of the daily deets! I bought a hidden camera. It's on my bow tie!
CLICK!
CLICK!
CLICK!

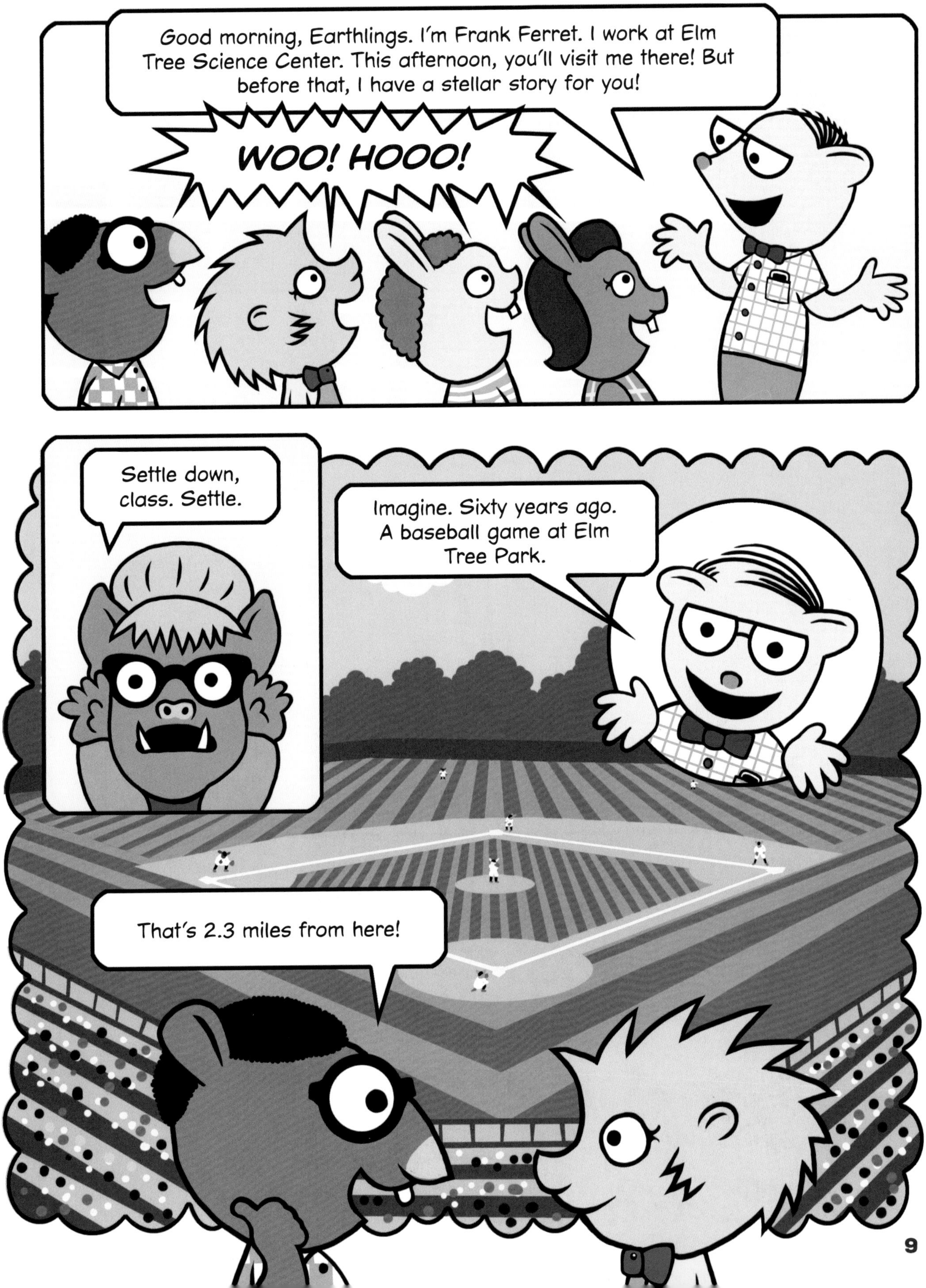
Good morning, Earthlings. I'm Frank Ferret. I work at Elm Tree Science Center. This afternoon, you'll visit me there! But before that, I have a stellar story for you!
WOO! HOOO!
Settle down, class. Settle.
Imagine. Sixty years ago. A baseball game at Elm Tree Park.
That's 2.3 miles from here!

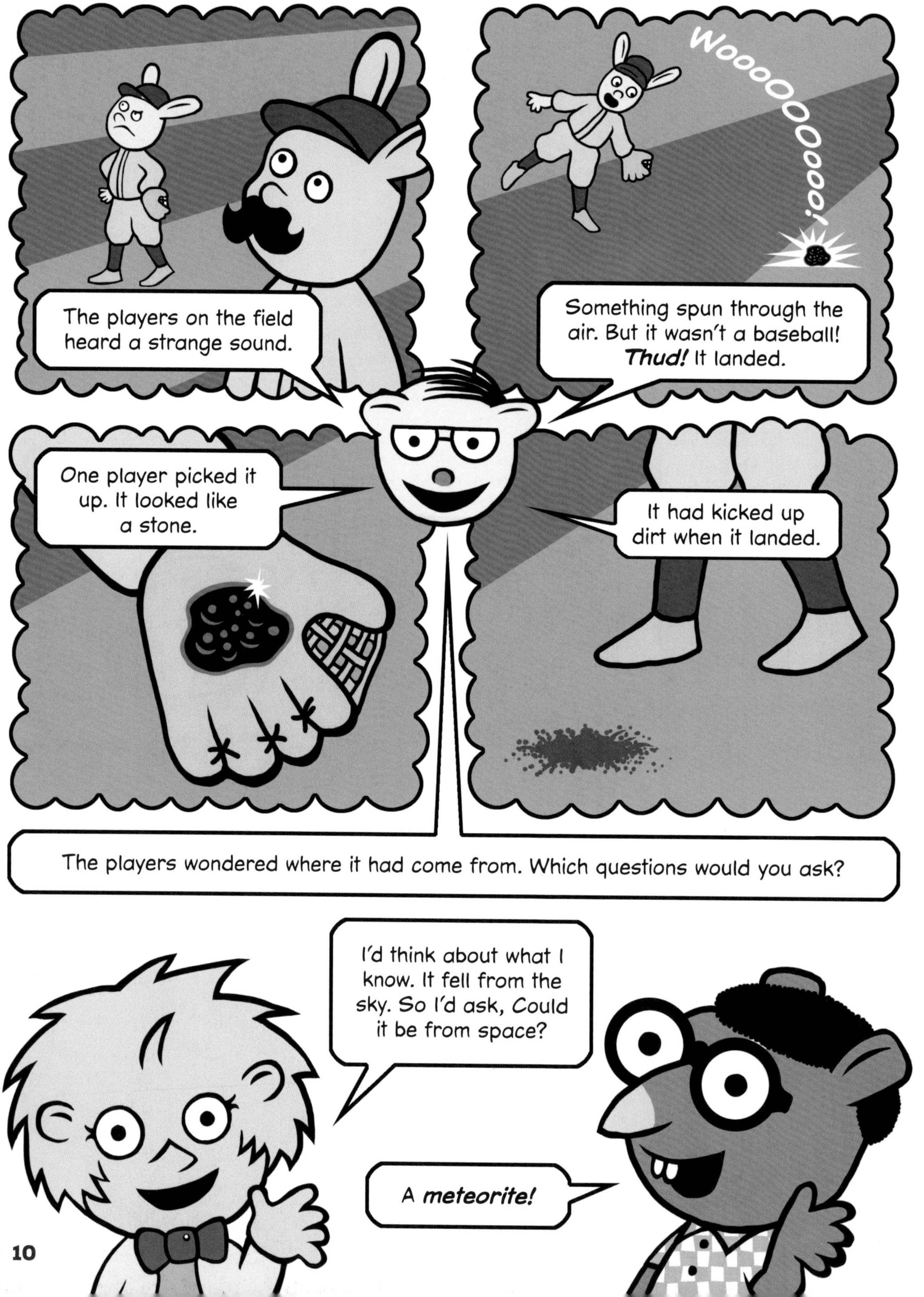
The players on the field heard a strange sound.
WoooOOOoooo!
Something spun through the air. But it wasn't a baseball! *Thud!* It landed.
One player picked it up. It looked like a stone.
It had kicked up dirt when it landed.
The players wondered where it had come from. Which questions would you ask?
I'd think about what I know. It fell from the sky. So I'd ask, Could it be from space?
A *meteorite!*

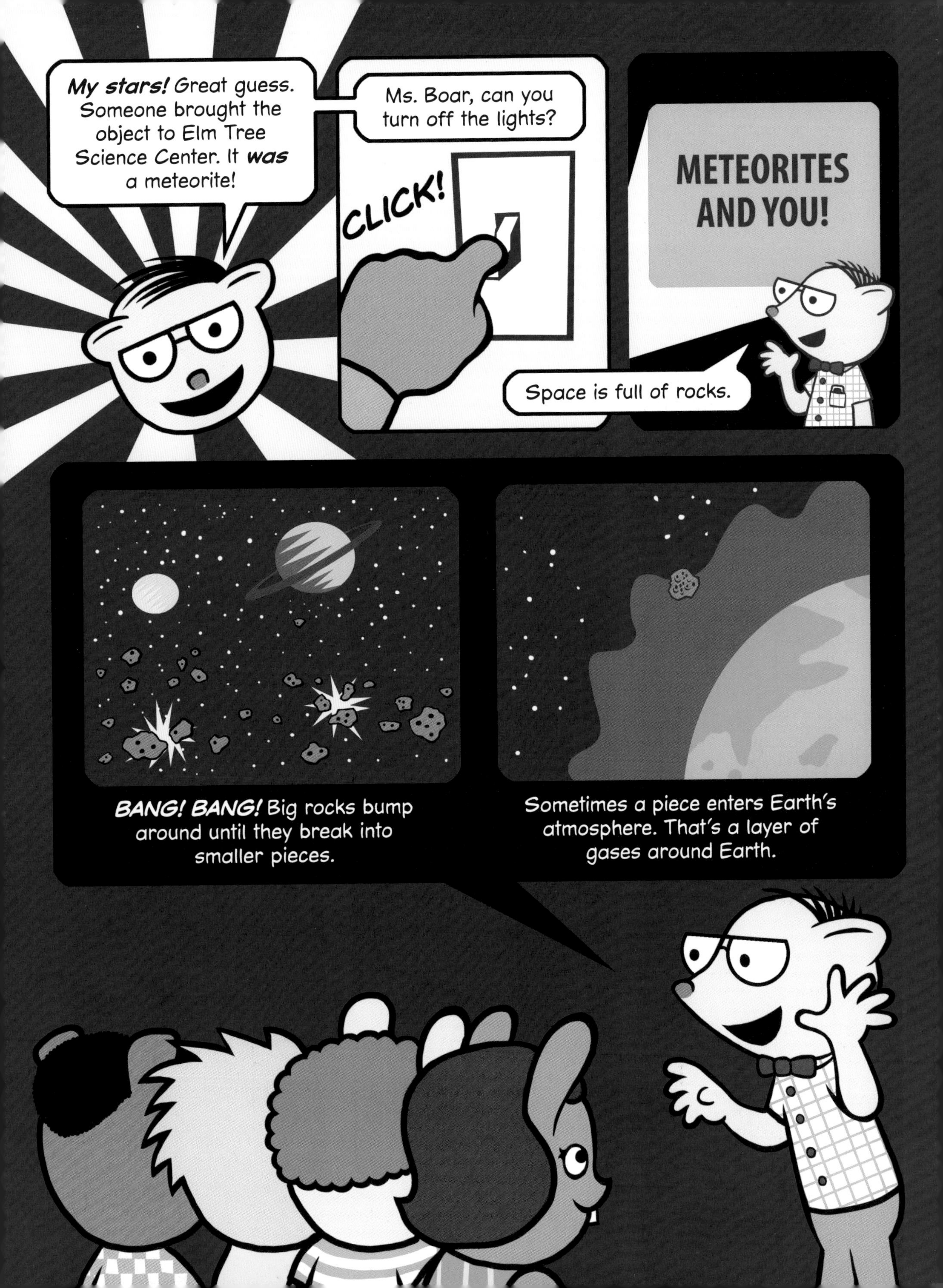

My stars! Great guess. Someone brought the object to Elm Tree Science Center. It was a meteorite!
Ms. Boar, can you turn off the lights?
CLICK!
METEORITES AND YOU!
Space is full of rocks.
BANG! BANG! Big rocks bump around until they break into smaller pieces.
Sometimes a piece enters Earth's atmosphere. That's a layer of gases around Earth.

The space rock speeds through the atmosphere. The thin outer layer of the rock heats up and melts off.

The melting part becomes the tail. It looks like a streak of light. It's called a meteor!

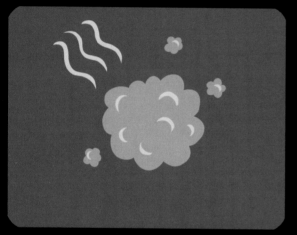

Sometimes the rest of the space rock burns up.

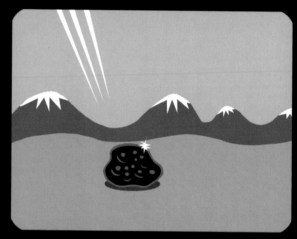

Sometimes it lands on Earth! *THUMP!* Now the rock is called a meteorite. Later, you'll get to see the one that landed in Elm Tree Park!

Woo! Hoo! Aaaah!

Cool! Yay!

CHAPTER THREE
Limburger-Rite or Limburger-Wrong?

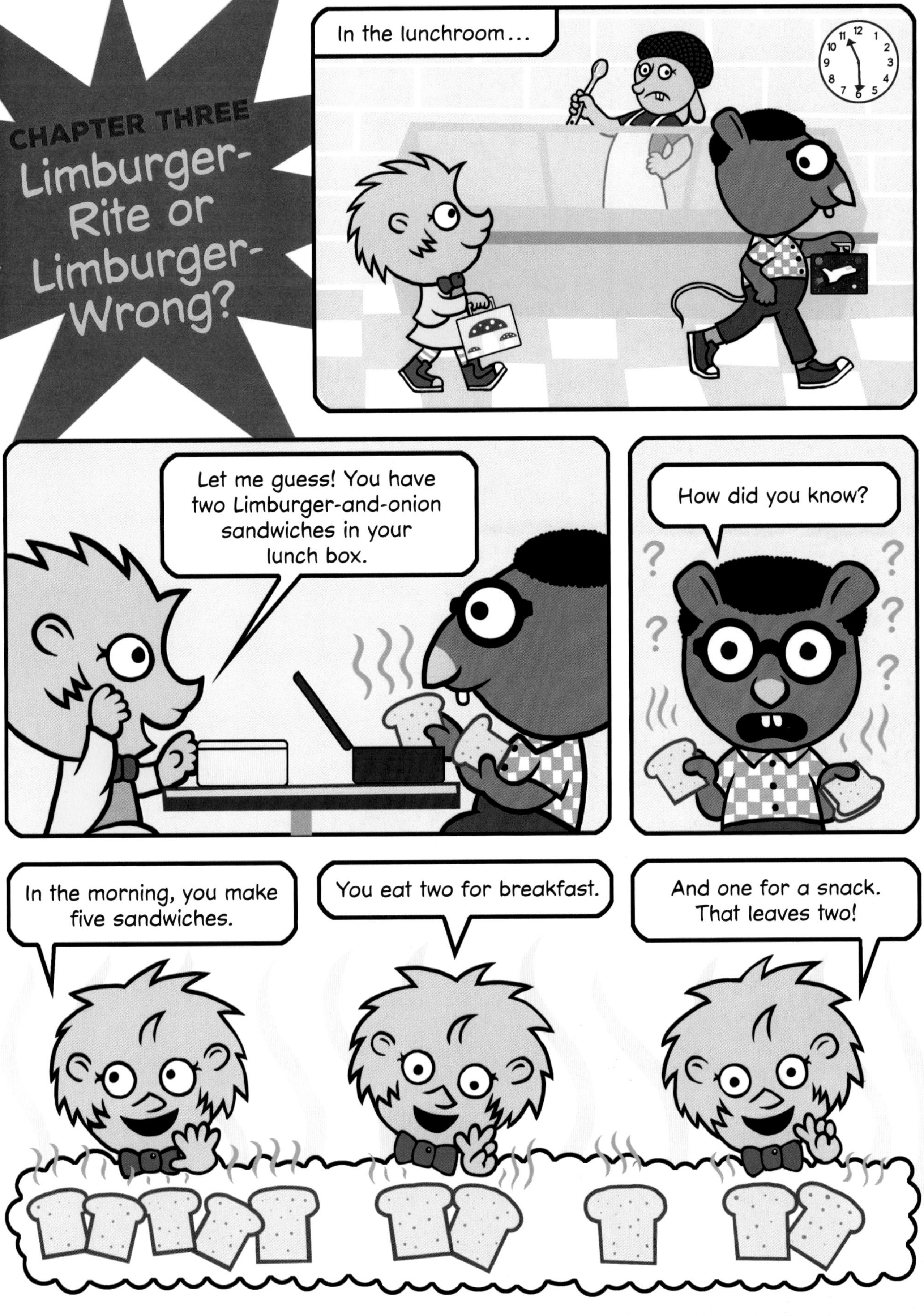
In the lunchroom...
Let me guess! You have two Limburger-and-onion sandwiches in your lunch box.
How did you know?
In the morning, you make five sandwiches.
You eat two for breakfast.
And one for a snack. That leaves two!

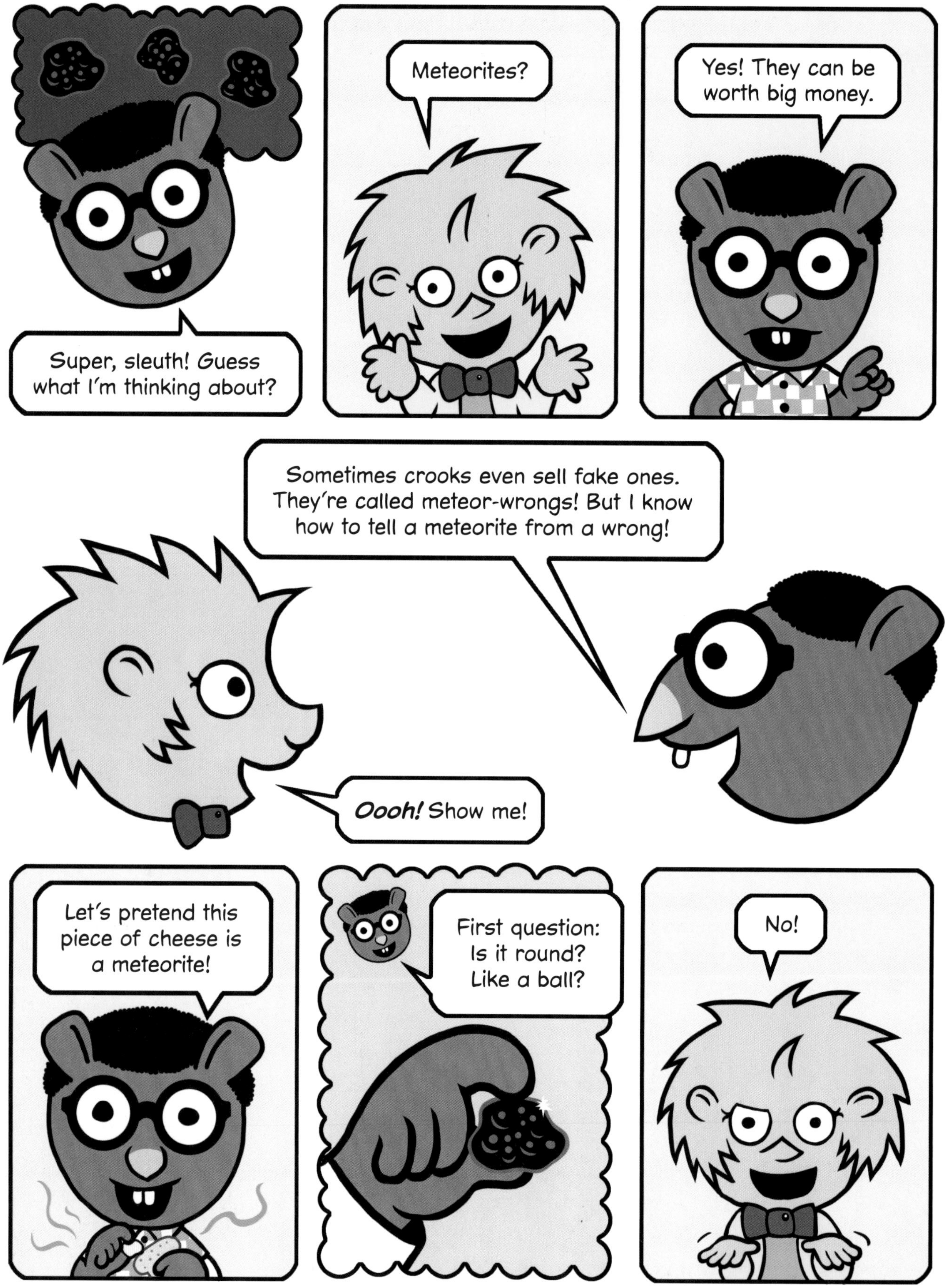
Super, sleuth! Guess what I'm thinking about?
Meteorites?
Yes! They can be worth big money.
Sometimes crooks even sell fake ones. They're called meteor-wrongs! But I know how to tell a meteorite from a wrong!
Oooh! Show me!
Let's pretend this piece of cheese is a meteorite!
First question: Is it round? Like a ball?
No!

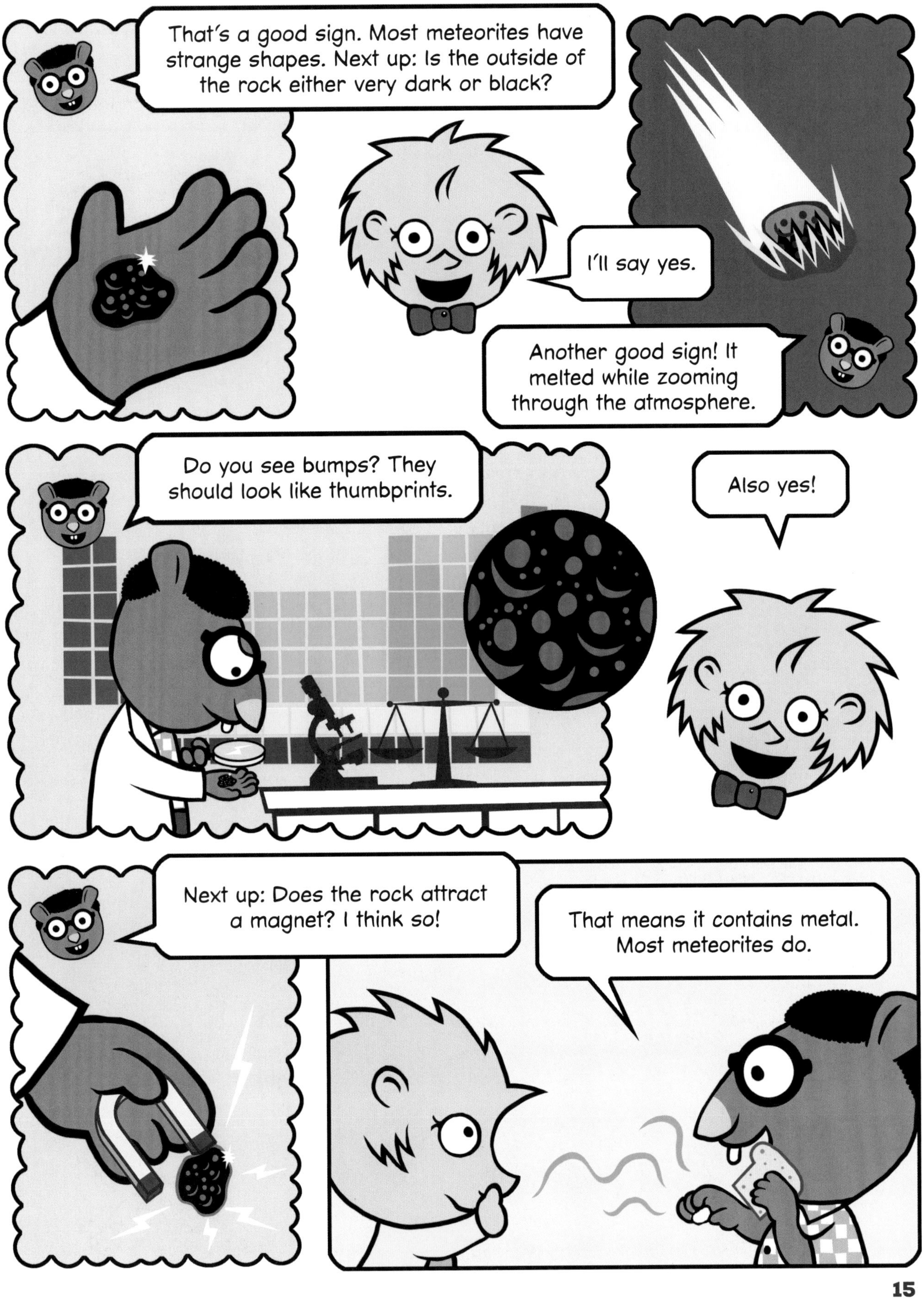
That's a good sign. Most meteorites have strange shapes. Next up: Is the outside of the rock either very dark or black?
I'll say yes.
Another good sign! It melted while zooming through the atmosphere.
Do you see bumps? They should look like thumbprints.
Also yes!
Next up: Does the rock attract a magnet? I think so!
That means it contains metal. Most meteorites do.

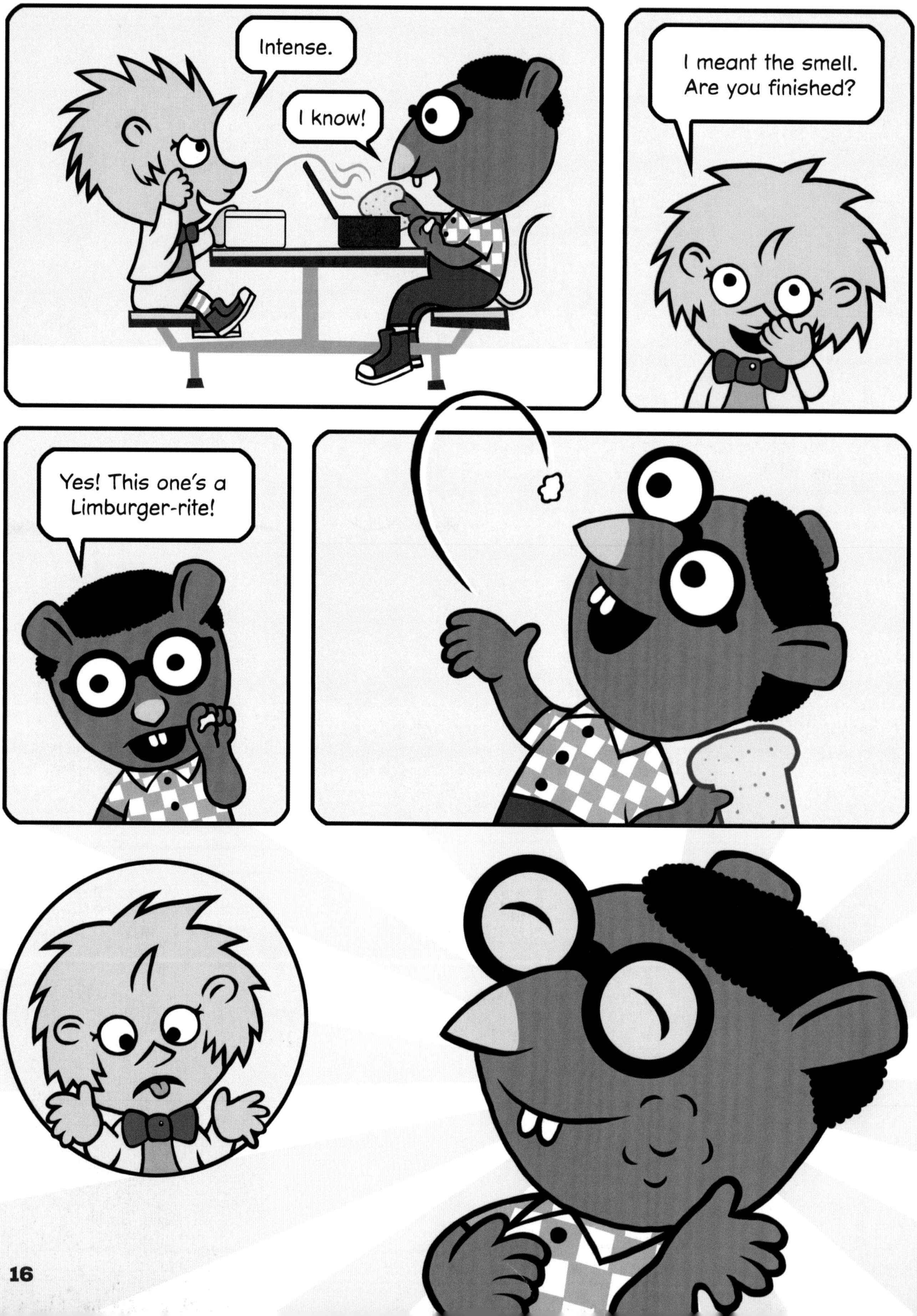
Intense.
I know!
I meant the smell. Are you finished?
Yes! This one's a Limburger-rite!

CHAPTER FOUR
The Elm Tree Park Meteorite

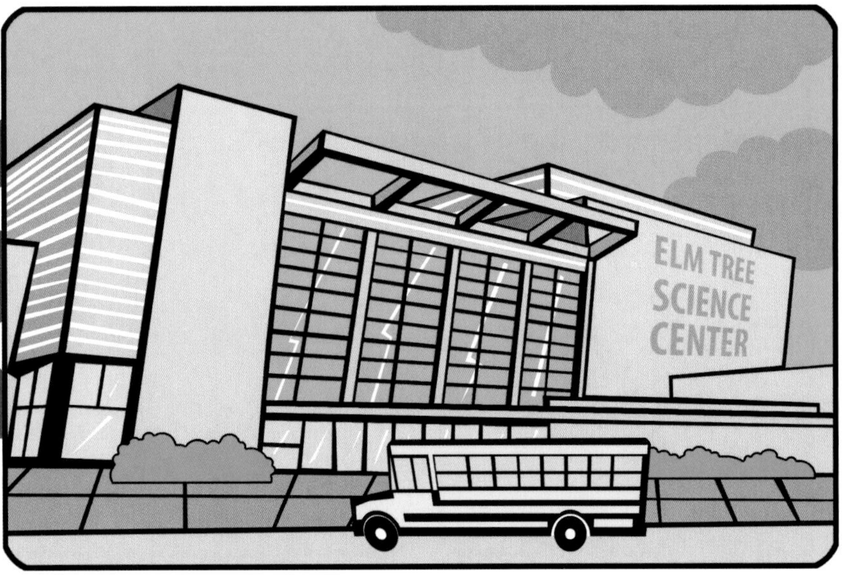
ELM TREE
SCIENCE
CENTER

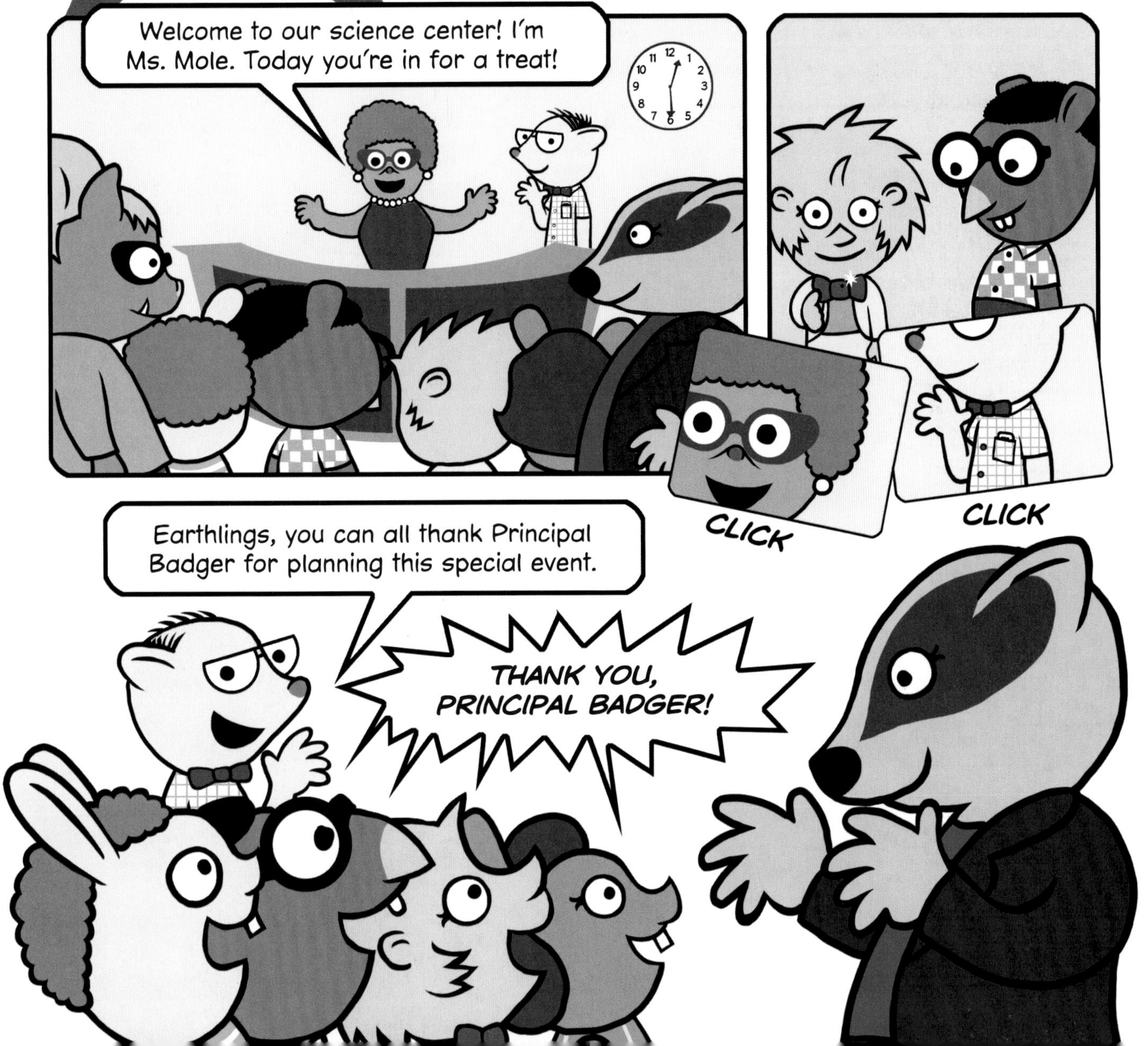
Welcome to our science center! I'm Ms. Mole. Today you're in for a treat!
CLICK
CLICK
Earthlings, you can all thank Principal Badger for planning this special event.
THANK YOU, PRINCIPAL BADGER!

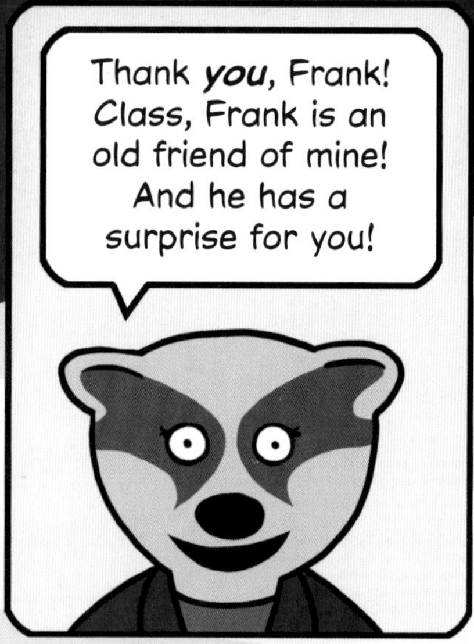
Thank *you*, Frank! Class, Frank is an old friend of mine! And he has a surprise for you!

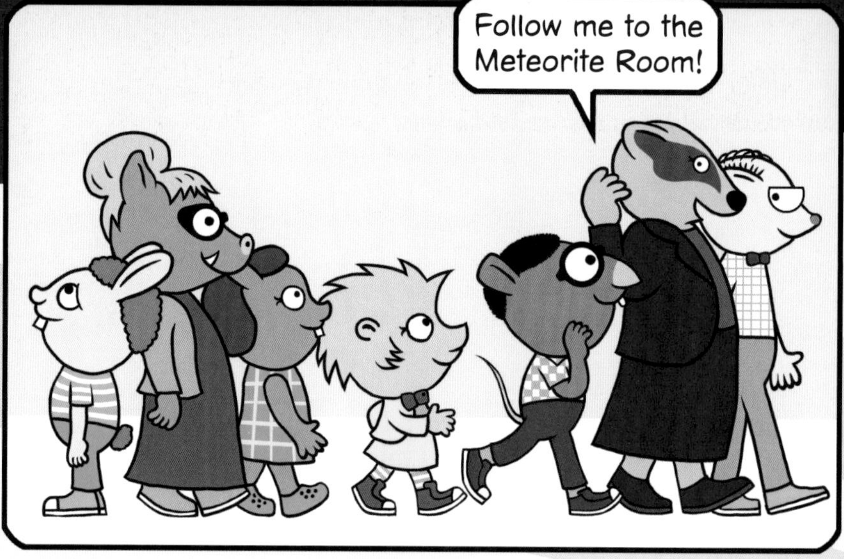
Follow me to the Meteorite Room!

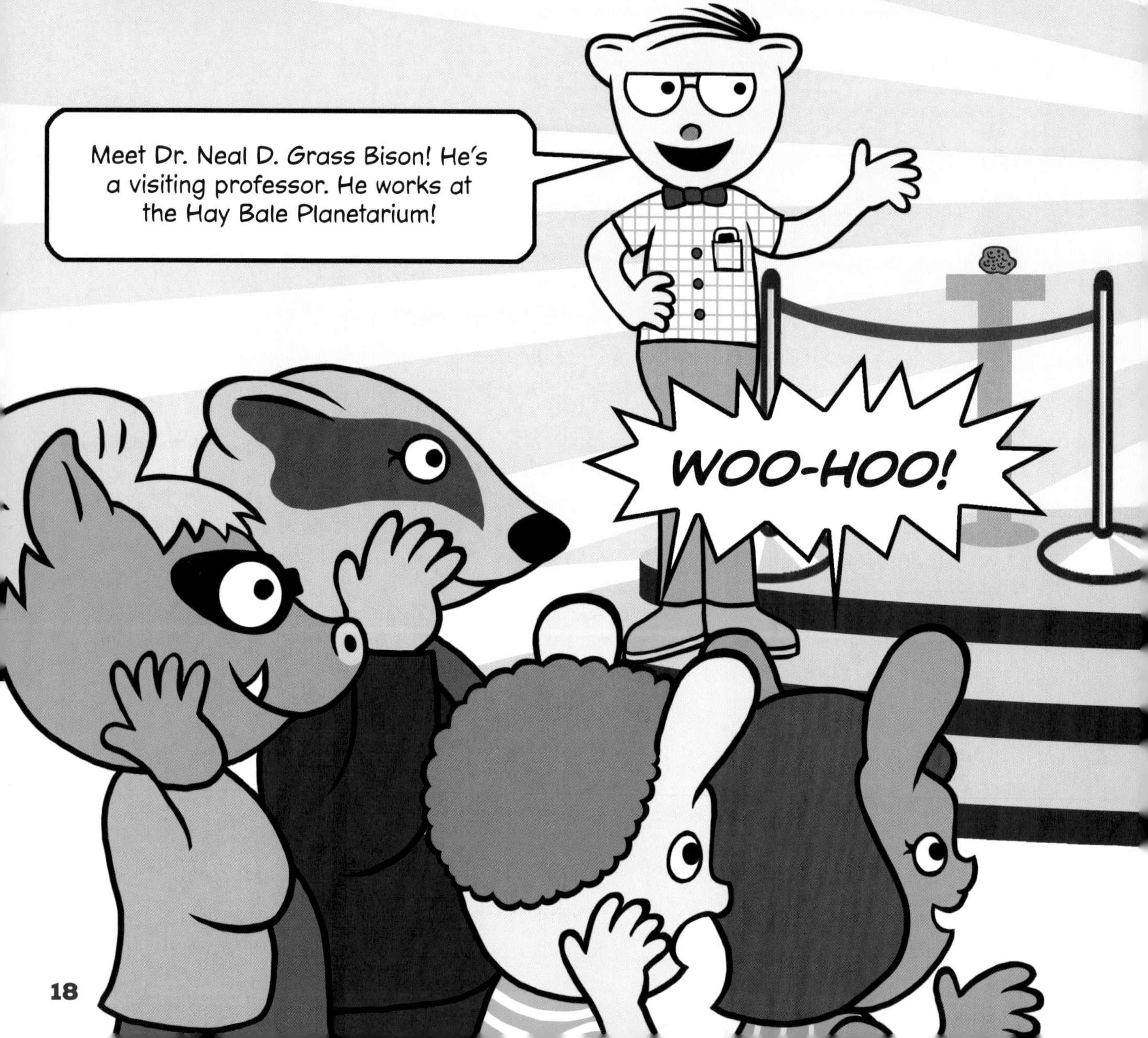
Meet Dr. Neal D. Grass Bison! He's a visiting professor. He works at the Hay Bale Planetarium!
WOO-HOO!

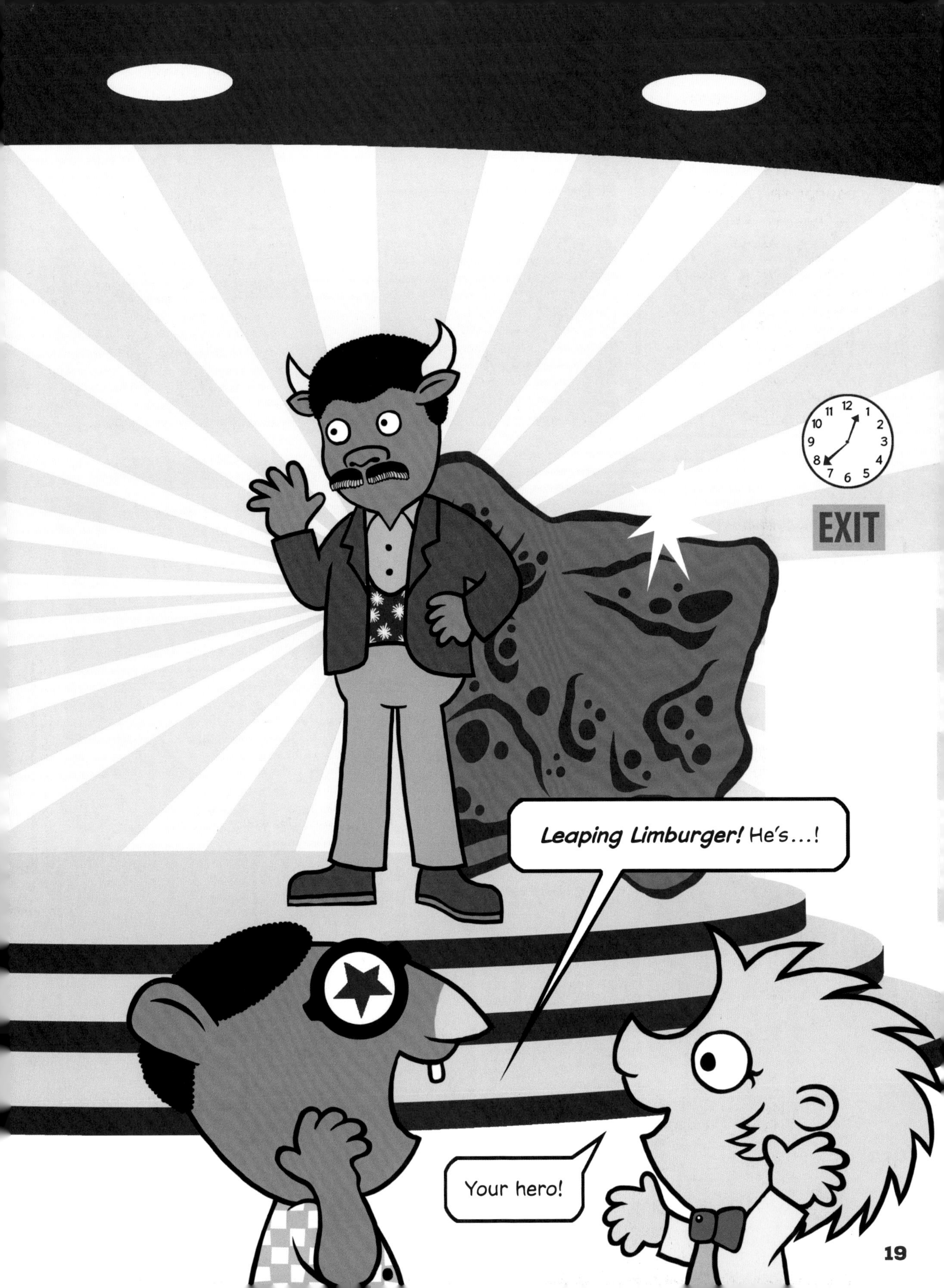
EXIT
Leaping Limburger! He's...!
Your hero!

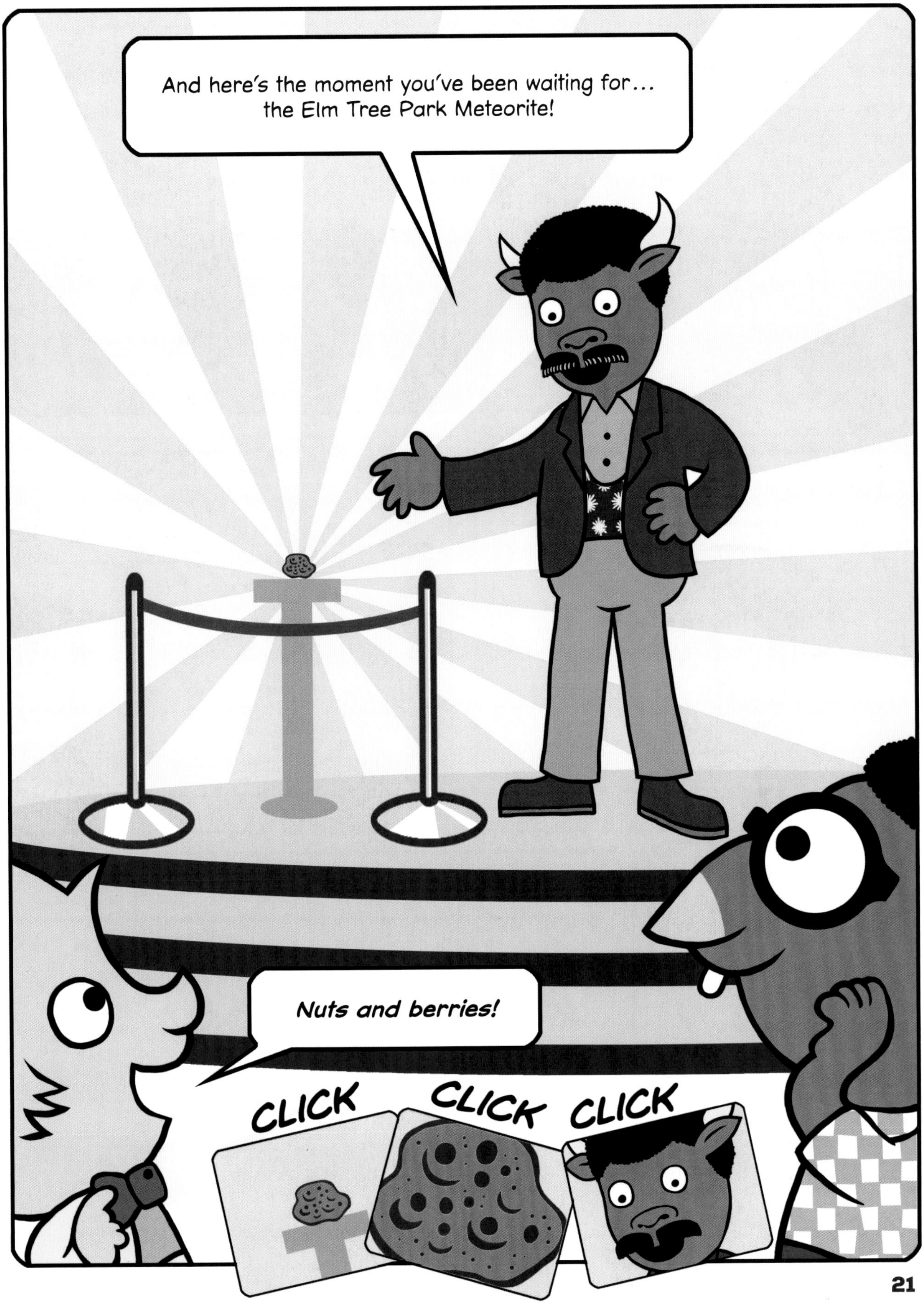
And here's the moment you've been waiting for... the Elm Tree Park Meteorite!
Nuts and berries!
CLICK
CLICK
CLICK

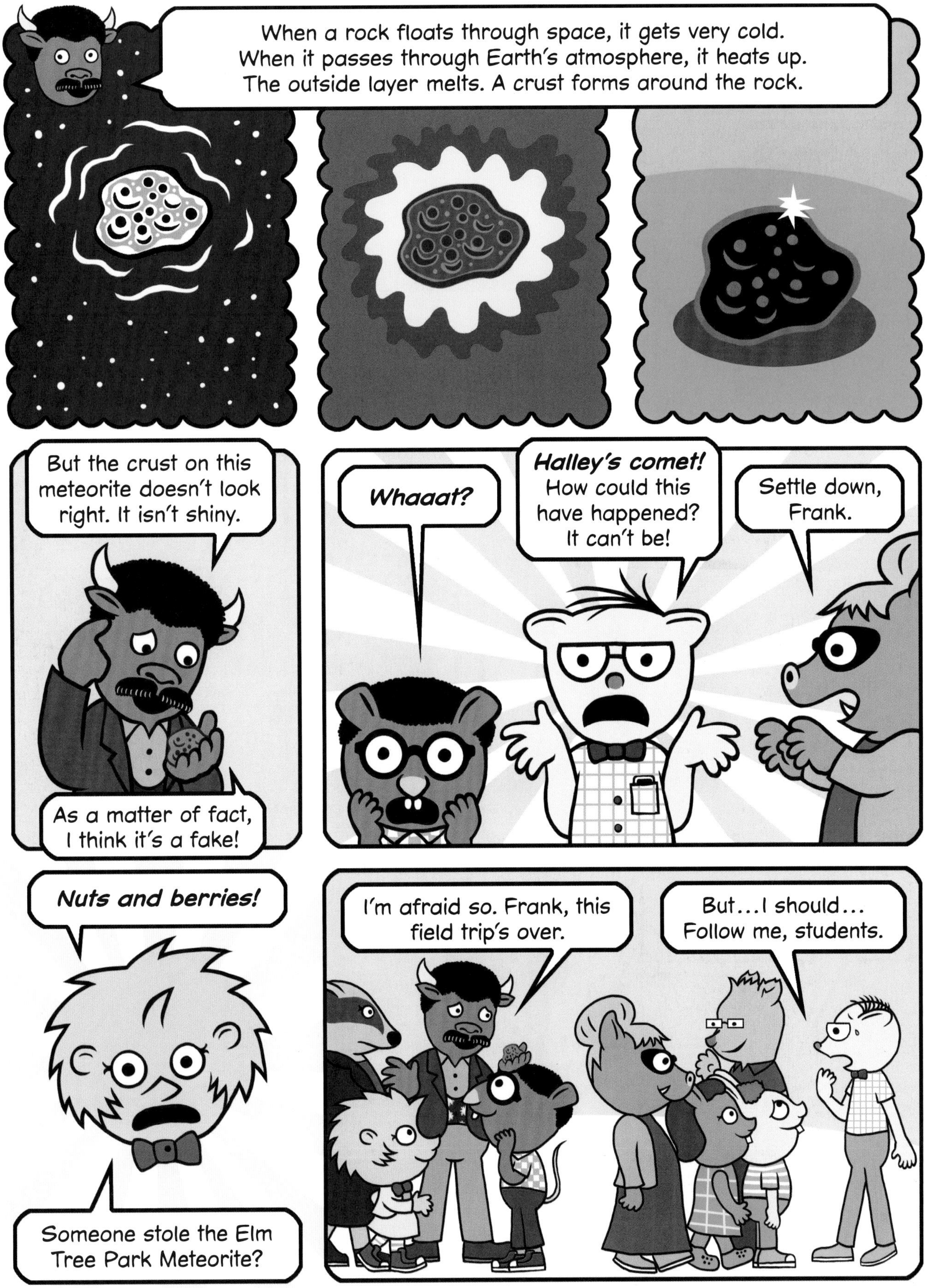

When a rock floats through space, it gets very cold. When it passes through Earth's atmosphere, it heats up. The outside layer melts. A crust forms around the rock.
But the crust on this meteorite doesn't look right. It isn't shiny.
As a matter of fact, I think it's a fake!
Whaaat?
Halley's comet! How could this have happened? It can't be!
Settle down, Frank.
Nuts and berries!
Someone stole the Elm Tree Park Meteorite?
I'm afraid so. Frank, this field trip's over.
But...I should... Follow me, students.

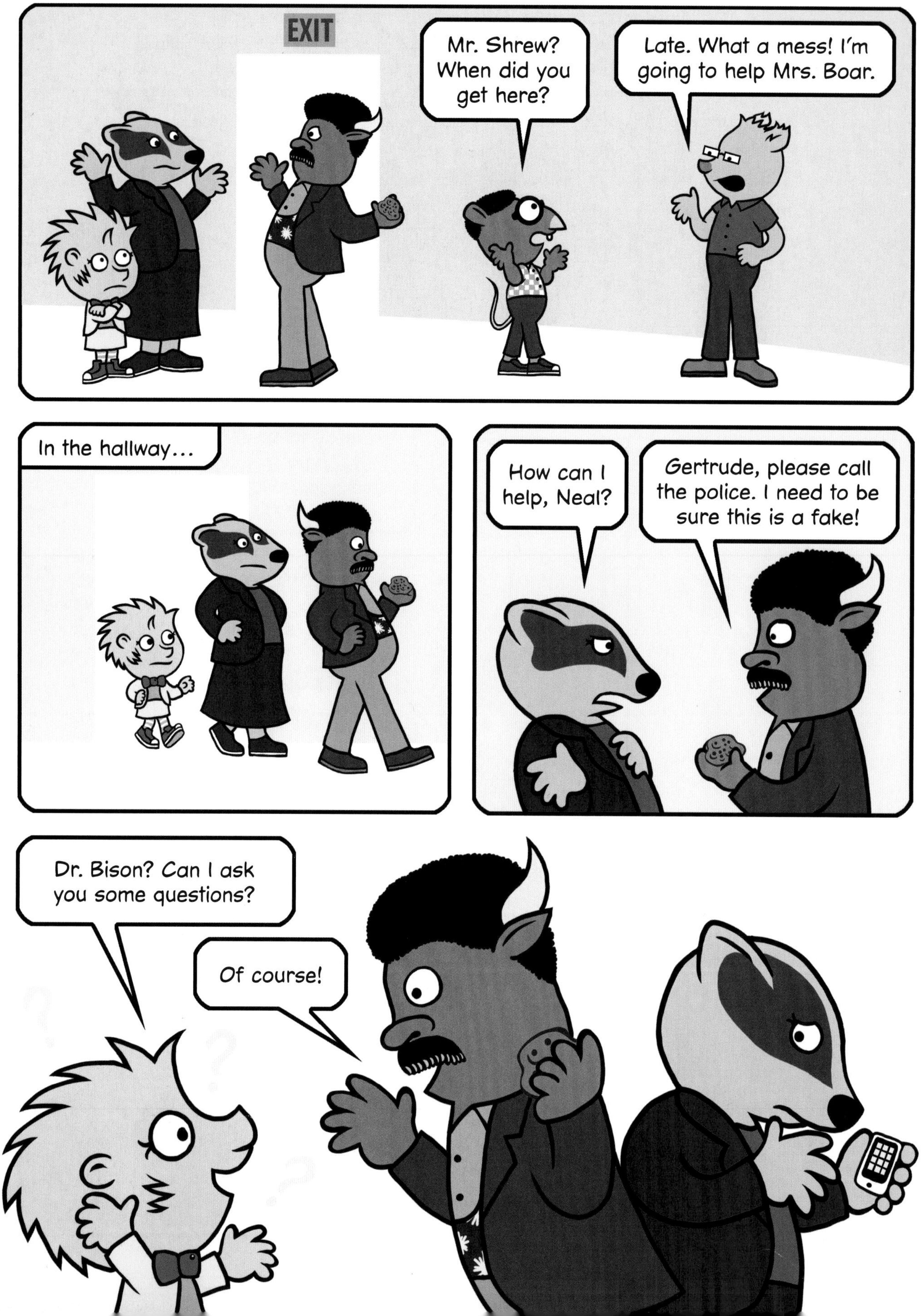
EXIT
Mr. Shrew? When did you get here?
Late. What a mess! I'm going to help Mrs. Boar.
In the hallway...
How can I help, Neal?
Gertrude, please call the police. I need to be sure this is a fake!
Dr. Bison? Can I ask you some questions?
Of course!

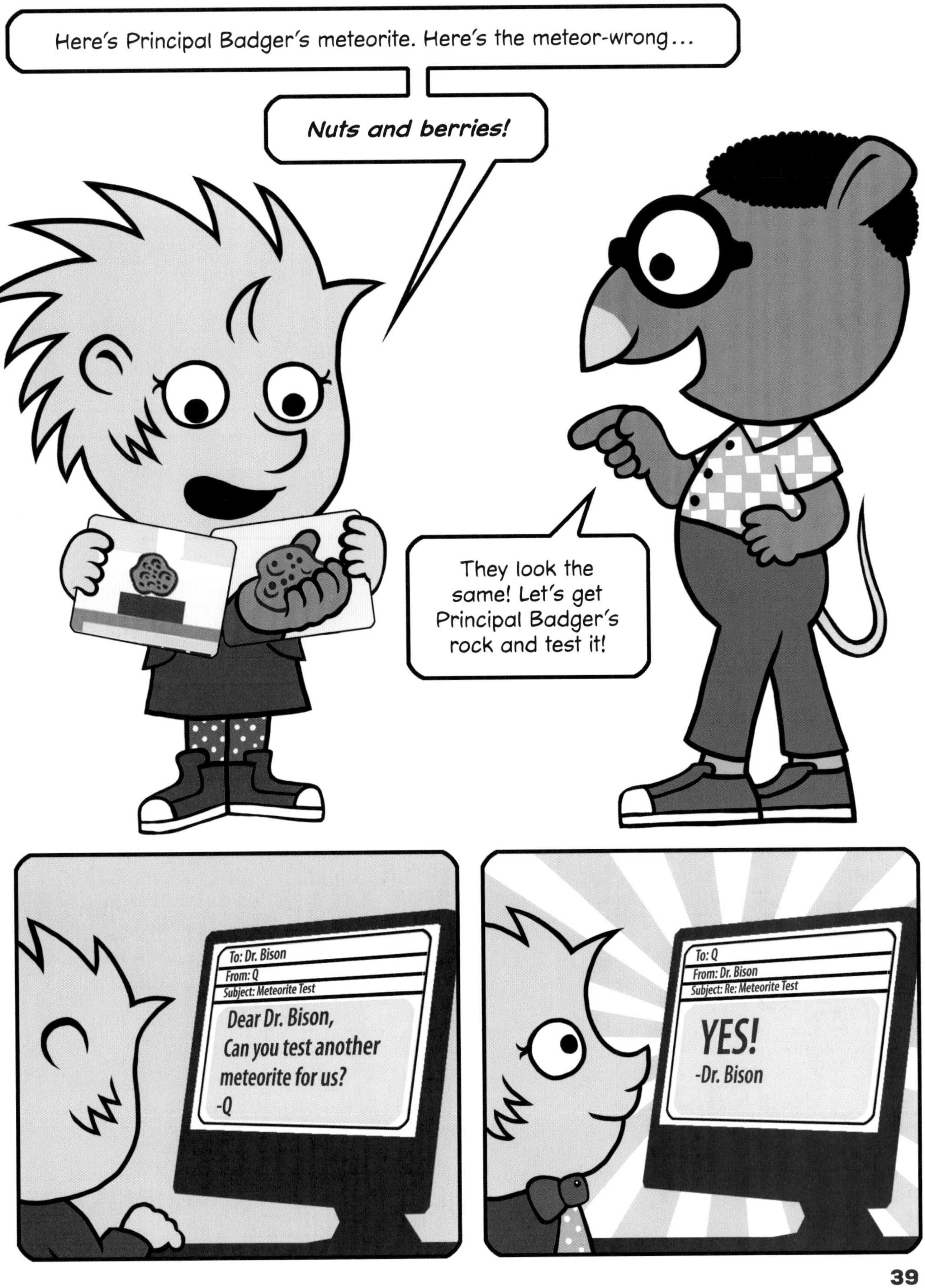
Here's Principal Badger's meteorite. Here's the meteor-wrong...
Nuts and berries!
They look the same! Let's get Principal Badger's rock and test it!
To: Dr. Bison
From: Q
Subject: Meteorite Test
Dear Dr. Bison,
Can you test another meteorite for us?
-Q
To: Q
From: Dr. Bison
Subject: Re: Meteorite Test
YES!
-Dr. Bison

Rock Stars

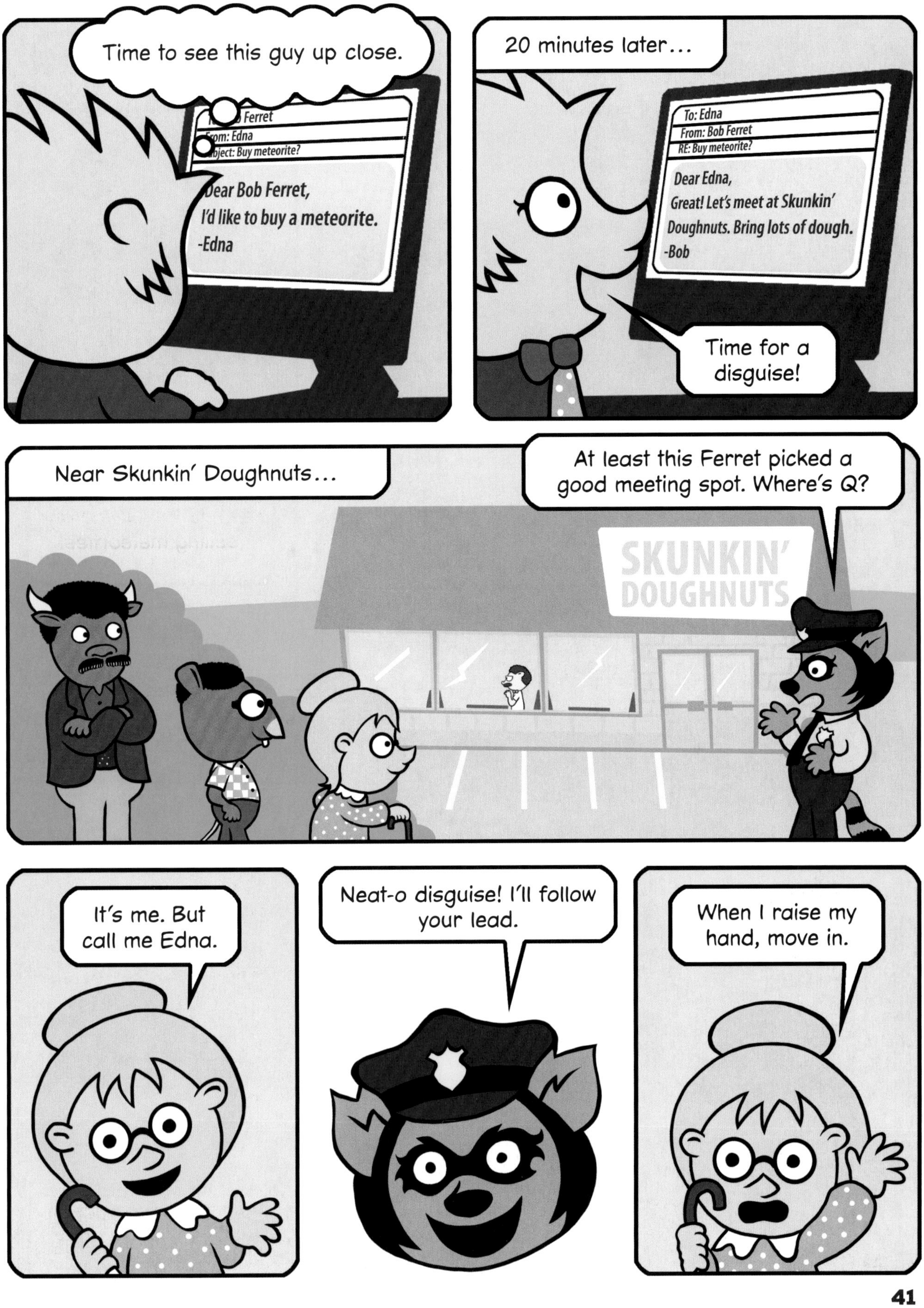
Time to see this guy up close.
Dear Bob Ferret,
I'd like to buy a meteorite.
-Edna
20 minutes later…
To: Edna
From: Bob Ferret
RE: Buy meteorite?
Dear Edna,
Great! Let's meet at Skunkin' Doughnuts. Bring lots of dough.
-Bob
Time for a disguise!
Near Skunkin' Doughnuts…
At least this Ferret picked a good meeting spot. Where's Q?
SKUNKIN' DOUGHNUTS
It's me. But call me Edna.
Neat-o disguise! I'll follow your lead.
When I raise my hand, move in.

43

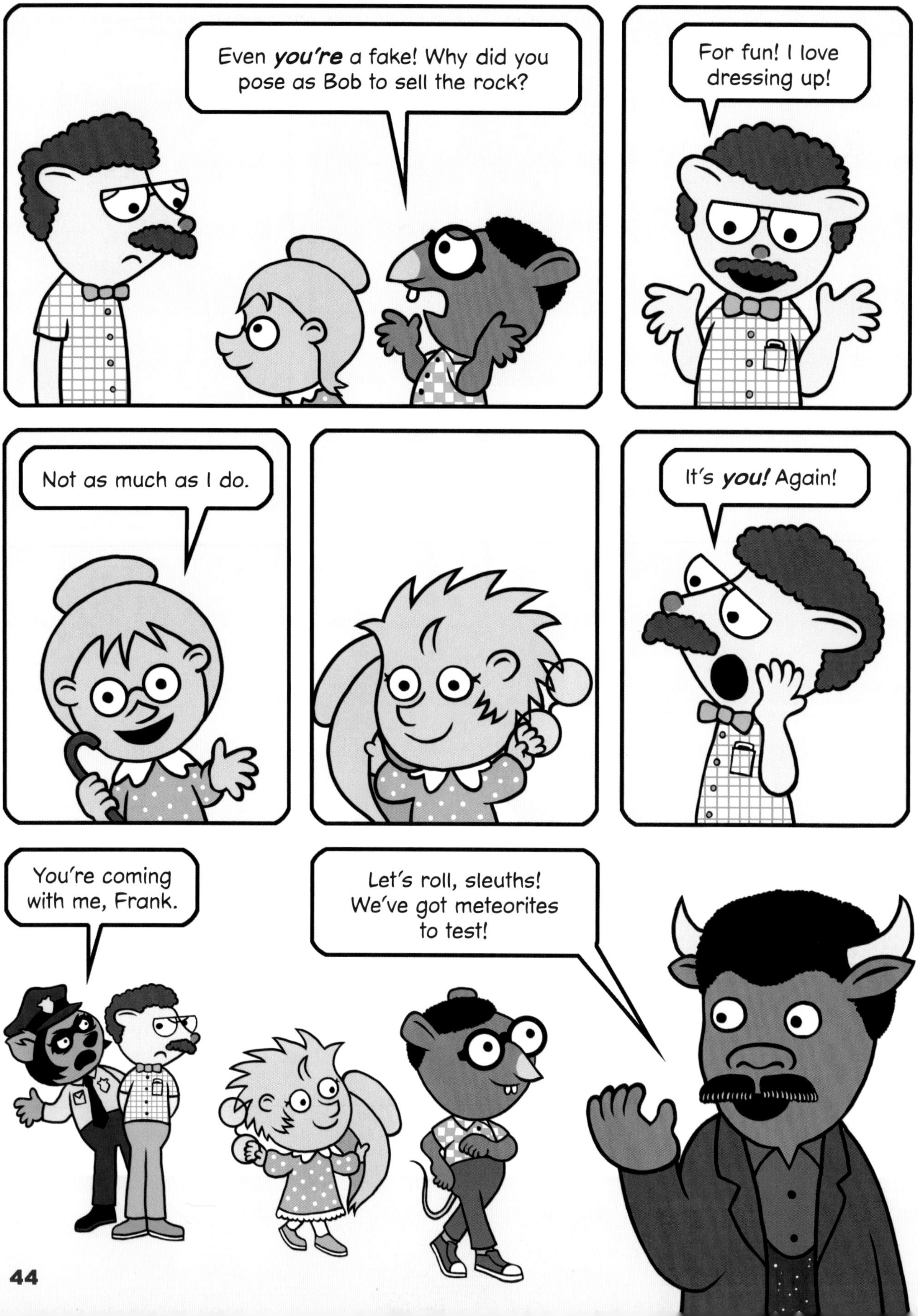
Even you're a fake! Why did you pose as Bob to sell the rock?
For fun! I love dressing up!
Not as much as I do.
It's you! Again!
You're coming with me, Frank.
Let's roll, sleuths! We've got meteorites to test!

ABOUT THE AUTHOR

Trisha Speed Shaskan has written more than forty books for children, including the Q & Ray series and *Punk Skunks*, both of which are illustrated by her husband, Stephen Shaskan. Several years ago, she watched the Perseid meteor shower and knew someday she'd write a story inspired by it. While writing this book, Trisha loved learning about meteors and meteorites. She hopes you enjoy it too! Visit her at trishaspeedshaskan.com.

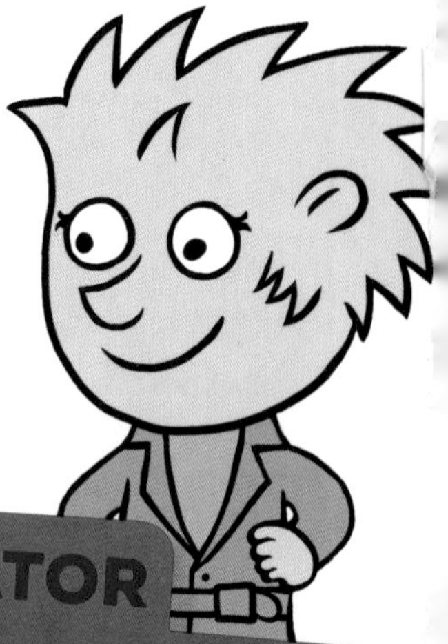

ABOUT THE ILLUSTRATOR

Stephen Shaskan is the author and the illustrator of *Big Choo*, *A Dog Is a Dog*, *Max Speed*, *Toad on the Road: A Cautionary Tale*, and *The Three Triceratops Tuff*. He's also the illustrator of *Punks Skunks* and the Q & Ray books. He is super excited to be creating this graphic novel series, since he grew up collecting, reading, and drawing comic books. Stephen and Trisha live in Minneapolis, Minnesota, with their cat, Eartha, and dog, Bea. Visit him at stephenshaskan.com.

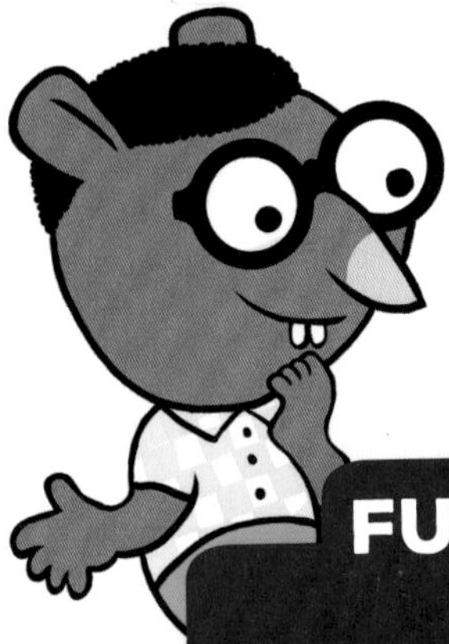

FUN FACTS

There's much more information about meteorites to explore! Many meteors don't make it to Earth. They heat up in the planet's atmosphere. Then they vaporize. That means they turn into gas.

Most of the meteorites that do fall to Earth are the size of specks of dust. But even large meteorites are hard to find. People who try to spot them go by the name chasers. Since 1980, only about one meteorite has been discovered in the United States each year.